THE HIGH HILLS

WILFRED'S MOUNTAIN ADVENTURE

JILL BARKLEM

CARNIVAL

For Peter

This edition published in 2000 by Diamond Books
77-85 Fulham Palace Road
Hammersmith, London, W68JB
First published in hardback in Great Britain
by HarperCollins Publishers Ltd in 1986
First published in paperback in 1996
3 5 7 9 10 8 6 4 2
Text and illustrations © Jill Barklem 1986
A CIP catalogue record for this title is available from the British Library.
The author asserts the moral right to be identified as the author of the work.
ISBN: 0 00 761010 6
Printed and bound in Italy

Brambly Hedge

For many generations, families of mice have made their homes in the roots and trunks of the trees of Brambly Hedge. If you are ever lucky enough to be nearby, you may see a wisp of smoke from a small chimney or even a steep flight of stairs deep within the trunk of a tree.

Mrs Apple

The mice of Brambly Hedge lead busy lives. They make all their own food and during the fine weather, they collect herbs,

Mr Apple

fruits and nuts from the hedge and surrounding fields. They then prepare delicious jams, pickles and preserves that are kept safely in the Store Stump where Mr Apple is the Warden. Mr Apple's wife, Mrs Apple, is the very best of cooks and their home, Crabapple Cottage, is always filled with the aroma of cakes and freshly baked bread.

Although the mice work hard, they always have time for fun. They welcome the opportunity to meet and celebrate and their favourite place for a party is the Old Oak Palace. This is where Lord and

Primrose

Lady Woodmouse live with their young daughter Primrose.

Lord & Lady Woodmouse

Primrose's best friend is Wilfred Toadflax who lives in the hornbeam tree at the end of the Hedge. Wilfred and his brother Teasel love to play tricks on their sisters Catkin and Clover.

These are just a few of the mice that live in the Hedge. Meet some of their friends and relatives in *The High Hills*.

Wilfred

It was the very end of autumn. The weather was damp and chilly and Wilfred was spending the day inside with the weavers. *Clickety, clack* went the loom, *whirr, whirr* went the spinning wheel. Lily and Flax were in a hurry.

"We must finish in time," said Flax. "We promised Mr Apple."

"What are you making?" asked Wilfred.

"Blankets," replied Lily.

"Who are they for?" said Wilfred.

"They are for the voles in the High Hills," replied Flax. "They have just discovered that the moths have eaten all their quilts and they've no time to make new ones before the cold weather comes. They're too busy gathering stores for winter. We're helping out."

"Can I help too?" asked Wilfred.

"That's kind of you, Wilfred, but not just now," said Lily. "Why don't you find yourself a book to read while I finish spinning this wool?"

Wilfred went over to the bookcase. On a shelf, tucked between volumes on dyestuffs and weaves, he found a thick book called *Daring Explorers of Old Hedge Days*. He settled himself comfortably and began to turn the pages.

"Sir Hogweed Horehound," he read, "determined to conquer the highest peak of the High Hills, for there, he knew, he would discover gold. Alone he set forth, taking in his trusty pack all he needed to survive the rigorous journey. . ."

Wilfred sat entranced. The whirr of the spinning wheel became the swish of eagles' wings, the clatter of the loom, the sound of falling rock, and the drops of rain on the window, jewels from the depths of some forgotten cave. Was there really gold in the hills beyond Brambly Hedge, he wondered.

Suddenly a door slammed. It was his mother come to fetch him home for tea.

"I hope he hasn't been too much trouble," said Mrs Toadflax.

"He has been so quiet, we'd almost forgotten he was here," said Lily. "You can send him down again tomorrow if you like."

Lily and Flax were already hard at work when Wilfred arrived the next morning. He settled down by the window again to read about Sir Hogweed Horehound and his intrepid search for gold.

The morning flew past and by the time Mr Apple arrived to collect Wilfred, Flax and Lily had almost finished the cloth.

"I'm sorry we couldn't match the yellow," said Flax. "We've used the last of Grandpa Blackthorn's lichen and no other dye will do."

"Never mind," said Mr Apple. "It's the blankets they need. We'll take them up to the hills tomorrow."

"The hills," repeated Wilfred. "Are you really going up to the High Hills?"

"Yes," replied Mr Apple. "Why?"

"Can I come?" Wilfred asked desperately. "Please say I can."

"Oh, I don't think so," said Mr Apple. "It's too far. We shall have to stay overnight."

"I'll be very good," urged Wilfred.

Mr Apple relented. "We'll see if your mother agrees," he said. "Come on, young mouse. It's time to go home."

To Wilfred's surprise, his mother did agree.

"It will do him good to be in the open air," she said.
Wilfred rushed upstairs to pack. He knew just what
he would need. Sir Hogweed Horehound had listed
all the essential gear in his book: rope, a whistle, food,
firesticks, cooking pots, a groundsheet and blankets,
a spoon, a water bottle and a first-aid kit.

"And I had better have a special bag for the gold,"
said Wilfred to himself as he gathered everything together.

He went to bed straight after supper. It was a long way
to the High Hills and to get to the Voles' Hole by dusk,
they would have to make an early start.

Next morning, soon after dawn, Flax, Lily and
Mr Apple called for Wilfred. They were carrying packs
on their backs, full of cloth and blankets, and there was
honey and cheese and a pudding for the voles from
Mrs Apple. Wilfred hurried down the stairs.

"Whatever have you got there?" asked Flax.

"It's my essential gear," explained Wilfred.

"You won't be needing a cooking pot. I've got some
sandwiches," said Mr Apple.

"But I must take everything," said Wilfred. His lip
began to quiver. "How can I find gold without my
equipment?"

"You'll have to carry it then," said Mr Apple. "We can't
manage any more."

The first part of the journey was easy. The four mice went up the hedge, past Crabapple Cottage, the Store Stump and Old Oak Palace. Then they rounded the weavers' cottages and arrived at the bank of the stream. Carefully they picked their way over the stepping stones and clambered up into the buttercup meadow.

Wilfred strode through the grass, occasionally lifting his paw to gaze at the distant peaks. Beyond the bluebell woods he could see the path begin to climb.

Mr Apple looked back. "How's my young explorer?" he said. "Ready for lunch?"

"Oh, please," said Wilfred, easing off his pack with relief.

The mice ate their picnic and enjoyed the late autumn sunshine but soon it was time to go on. All through the afternoon they walked. The path became steeper and steeper, and when they looked behind them, they could see the fields and woods and hedges spread out far below.

By tea-time, it was getting dark and cold, and the hills around were shrouded in mist. At last they saw a tiny light shining from a rock beneath an old hawthorn tree.

"Here we are," said Mr Apple. "Knock on the door, Wilfred, will you?"

An elderly vole opened it a crack. When she saw Mr Apple, she cried, "Pip! Fancy you climbing all this way, and with your bad leg too."

"We couldn't leave you without blankets, now could we," said Mr Apple.

The mice crowded into the cottage and were soon sitting round the fire, drinking hot bilberry soup and resting their weary paws.

For Wilfred, the conversation came and went in drifts and soon he was fast asleep. Someone lifted him gently onto a little bracken bed in the corner and the next thing he knew was the delicious smell of breakfast, sizzling on the range.

Wilfred ate heartily, oatcakes with rowanberry jelly, and listened to the voles describing their hard life in the hills. He was disappointed when Mr Apple announced that it was time to leave.

"Can't we explore a bit first?" he begged.

"Flax and I have to get back to work," said Lily, "but why don't you two follow on later?"

"Well," relented Mr Apple, "there are some fine junipers beyond the crag. . ."

"And Mrs Apple *loves* junipers," said Wilfred quickly, "let's get her some."

So the mice said goodbye to the voles and Mr Apple and Wilfred set off up the path.

Wilfred ran on ahead and was soon round the crag. When Mr Apple caught up with him, Wilfred was half way up a steep face of rock.

"Wilfred!" cried Mr Apple. "Come down."

"Just a minute," shouted Wilfred. "I've found something."

Mr Apple watched as Wilfred pulled himself up onto the narrow ledge and started scraping at the rock and stuffing something in his pocket.

"Look!" cried Wilfred. "Gold!"

"Don't be silly, Wilfred," shouted Mr Apple. "That's not gold. Come down at once."

Wilfred looked over the side. His voice faltered. "I can't," he said. "I'm scared."

Mr Apple was exasperated. "Wait there," he shouted. Slowly he climbed the steep rocks, carefully placing his paws in the clefts of the stones. The ledge was very narrow. "We'll edge along this way. Perhaps the two paths will meet," he said. "We certainly can't go down the way we came up."

As they walked cautiously along the ledge, an ominous mist began to rise from the valley.

"If only we had some rope," said Mr Apple. "We ought to rope ourselves together."

Wilfred put his paw in his pack and produced the rope! Mr Apple tied it carefully round Wilfred's middle

and then round his own. And it was just as well for a few minutes later they were engulfed in a thick white fog.

"Turn to the rock face, Wilfred, we'll ease our way along, one step at a time."

They went on for a long time, then they took a rest. As they sat on the wet rock, the mist parted for a few seconds, just long enough to show a deep strange valley below.

Mr Apple was worried. He had no idea where they were. It looked as though they would have to spend the night on the mountain. It would be very cold and dark, and all he had in his pocket were two sandwiches the voles had given him for the journey down. His leg was feeling stiff and sore too. What was to be done? He explained the situation to Wilfred.

"It's all my fault," said Wilfred, "I didn't mean us to get lost. I just wanted to find gold like Sir Hogweed."

"Never mind," said Mr Apple. "We must look for somewhere to spend the night."

A short way along the path, the ledge became a little wider. Under an overhang of rock a small cave ran back into the mountainside.

"Look," cried Wilfred, slinging his pack inside. "Base camp!"

Mr Apple sat gingerly on the damp moss at the mouth of the cave. Everything felt damp, his clothes, his whiskers, his handkerchief.

"I wish I'd brought my pipe, we could have made a fire," he sighed. "Never mind, we'll huddle close and try to keep warm."

But Wilfred was busily searching in his pack again. Out came the firesticks and the tinderbox. "I'll see if there's some dry wood at the back of the cave," he said enthusiastically.

"Wilfred," cried Mr Apple in admiration, "you're a real explorer."

Soon they had a cheerful blaze on the ledge outside the cave. Wilfred produced two blankets and the mice wrapped themselves up snugly while their clothes dried in front of the fire. The little kettle was filled from the water bottle and proudly Wilfred set out a feast of bread and cheese and honeycakes.

"You know," said Mr Apple, as he settled back against the rock, "I haven't enjoyed a meal so much for years."

To while away the time, Mr Apple began to tell Wilfred stories of his adventurous youth, and as they talked, the mists gradually cleared and a starry sky spread out above them. All was quiet but for the murmur of a stream which ran through the valley below like a silver ribbon in the moonlight. Warmed by the fire, they became drowsy and soon fell asleep.

The next morning they were woken by the sun shining into the cave.

"It's a beautiful day," called Wilfred, peering over the ledge, "and I can see a path down the mountain."

Mr Apple sat up and stretched his leg. It still hurt. "We'll have to go down slowly, I'm afraid," he said.

"Is it your leg?" said Wilfred. "I can help," and he brought out a jar of comfrey ointment from his first-aid kit.

They packed up and set off down the path. Mr Apple did the best he could but his leg was very painful. He managed to get as far as the stream but then he stopped and sat on a boulder with a sigh. "I can't go any further," he said. "What are we to do?"

The two mice sat in silence and watched the water swirl past the bank.

"Don't worry," said Wilfred, trying to be cheerful. "We'll think of something."

Suddenly he jumped up. "I've got it," he cried excitedly. "We'll *sail* down the stream!" He ran to the bank and with his ice-axe, he hooked out some large sticks that had caught behind a rock in the water. Using his rope to lash them together, he made a raft. "Come on," said Wilfred, "we'll shoot the rapids!"

"Are you sure this is a good idea?" said Mr Apple. "Wherever will we end up?"

"Don't worry," said Wilfred. "It's all going to be all right."

Carefully they climbed onto the raft, Mr Apple let go of the bank and they were off!

They were swept to the middle of the stream as it raced down the mountainside, twisting and turning, sweeping and splashing, careering over rocks and cutting through deep banks.

"My hat," shouted Wilfred. "I've lost my hat."

"Never mind that," cried Mr Apple, "just hold on tight. There's a boulder ahead."

Wilfred gripped the sides of the raft, and somehow they managed to keep the raft, and themselves, afloat.

Down by the stream, Dusty was ferrying a search party of mice over to the buttercup meadows when he suddenly caught sight of a small red hat floating along on the current.

"Look there," he shouted. All the mice peered over the side of the boat.

"It's Wilfred's hat," cried out Mrs Toadflax. "Whatever can have happened to him?"

"Can he swim?" asked Mrs Apple anxiously.

Meanwhile Wilfred and Mr Apple were beginning to enjoy their trip on the river. The ground had levelled out and the pace of the stream had become gentler. They looked about them with interest.

"Wilfred," called Mr Apple, "can you see what I can see? I'm sure that's our willow ahead."

Wilfred stared at the bank. "It is!" he yelled.

"And there's the Old Oak Palace and the hornbeam. This is *our* stream!"

As they rounded the bend, they saw the Brambly Hedge mice climbing out of Dusty's boat. At the very same moment, Mrs Apple looked up and cried, "Look! Look! There they are!"

The mice turned in amazement; the raft was almost abreast of them.

"Quick," shouted Dusty, "catch hold of this rope and I'll haul you to shore."

As the two mice clambered out of the raft and up onto the bank, they all hugged each other.

"Wilfred, you're safe," cried Mrs Toadflax.

"My dear, what has happened to your leg?" said Mrs Apple.

Lord Woodmouse took charge. "Come on, everybody," he said. "Let's get these travellers home and dry, and then we can hear the full story."

The mice made their way along the hedgerow to the hornbeam tree. Soon everybody was sitting round the fire, eating cake and drinking acorn coffee.

"Now tell us exactly what happened," urged Flax.

"Well, it was my fault," explained Wilfred again. "I was looking for gold and I got stuck. Mr Apple had to rescue me and then we got lost. And Mr Apple's leg hurt so much, we had to come back on the raft."

"Did you find any gold?" interrupted Primrose.

"No, only this silly old dust," said Wilfred, pulling the bag out of his pocket. Flax and Lily gasped.

"Wilfred! That's not dust. That's Grandpa Blackthorn's lichen. It's very rare. You *are* clever! Wherever did you find it?"

Primrose ran to fetch some paper and Wilfred proudly drew a map so that they could find the place again.

"And when we go, you shall come with us, Wilfred," promised Lily.

Mr Apple was tired and soon he and Mrs Apple
went home to Crabapple Cottage. One by one, the
visitors drifted away. It was time for the explorer to
go to bed.

Wilfred followed his mother up the stairs.

"What adventures!" she said, washing his face and
paws and helping him take off his muddy dungarees.

Wilfred climbed into bed. As his mother tucked
him in, he thought of his night beneath the stars and
snuggling down under his warm blankets, he was
soon fast asleep.